The Green Mountain Shaman

Written by Patsy Stanley

ISBN 9781732377974
ISBN E-book 9781732377981
ISBN Downloadable Audio 978173237298

LCCN 2018908973

The Green Mountain Shaman

An isolated, high mountain village of indigenous
people called the Mokie lose their Shaman. With
no Shaman to guide them, the Mokie abandon their
old ways while the young Mokie begin crossing the Green
Mountains and settling in the cities on the other side.
The Mokie left behind mourn their losses and stay
hopeless until a blizzard blows a black crow and an odd
stranger into their village. Is he the new Shaman they have
needed?

Patsy Stanley

Patsy Stanley is an artist, illustrator and author.
She has authored both nonfiction and fiction books
including novels, children's books, energy books,
art zines, and more. She may be found online
at Amazon.com, Barnes & Noble books,
and at fineartamerica.com.
She can reached at patsystanley123@gmail.
for questions and comments.

The Green Mountain Shaman is now available on
audio book!

Once upon a time, a small village of indigenous people called the Mokie, lived in a high mountain valley, far away from the rest of the world.

A cold, clear, wide stream of water ran through the middle of their high, hidden valley. The stream flowed under tall, green shade trees. It meandered through water reeds and curved bluely around sun warmed rocks, and danced above swaying, lacy green and purple grasses anchored by colorful pebbles. Fat, tasty fish jumped and swam in the deep, clean stream.

The valley floor was rich and fertile with the dark topsoil that had washed down from the mountains for thousands of years. The men, women and children in the village kept themselves busy with the needs of everyday life, just as their ancestors had done before them. They farmed the rich, dark soil of the flat, green, lush valley. They grew corn and beans and squash in the bright summer sunshine. They hunted in the cool, green forests on the tall mountains.

They built their homes with trees from the green forests and the red and yellow clay from the stream banks, and decorated them with smooth stones from the stream bed. They gathered herbs and fished and cleaned themselves, and played and swam in the mountain stream.

As they worked and played, their laughter bounced against the mountains and echoed back through their hidden valley. None of the Mokie ever thought about leaving the tall ring of green, tree covered mountains that hid their secluded home from the outside world. They were happy just the way they were, living in their lodges and watching the sun to keep the time, and having sleds to ride on and to carry things.

The Mokie were river people. They had always had a shaman to lead them and take care of their ills and interpret the world for them. Their Shaman invested meaning into their lives, and they relied on him to explain the mysteries that inevitably took place in life.

Their shaman did many things. He led the rituals that were a necessary part of their lives. He tended to their spiritual needs and answered their questions. He went into the green mountain forests surrounding the village and talked with the animals, and brought back their wisdom to the Mokie.

The shaman painted himself and danced around the fires at night and recited the stories of the people's ancestors, so they would remember their lineage and history and keep their roots.

2

And so it was that the shaman watched the moon changes, and led the people to the fire in the sacred circle in the center of the village during the large summer moon so they could dance and feast.

Each season was strong in the little hidden valley high in the green mountains. When the first snow began to fall, the Mokie were ready. They retreated into their lodges and lit their fires and checked their supplies of dried foods and the root vegetables they had stored in their lodge cellars.

The long winter months settled in. The Shaman led the Mokie People to the fire in the central lodge at the large winter moon so they could drum and rattle and sing songs, and tell of their ancestor's journeys through many past winter seasons.

Some stories named the ancestors who had been lost to blizzards while out in the mountains hunting for food when the Mokie People had had bad growing seasons and gone hungry. In those times, they hadn't been able to store up enough food to keep them through the winter.

In happier stories, the stream had frozen solid, and they had skated on it in homemade shoes, and built a fire nearby to warm up at.

There were fall and winter children born, and the Mokie people laughed about the differences between them and the spring and summer children.

Through their songs and stories, the Mokie stayed wise about their strengths and weaknesses. At the gatherings, they spoke of the past, and what was happening to them now. They spoke of the future, the things they were afraid of, and the things they were proud of. The shaman listened and helped them find the good meanings in life, and let the bad ones go.

The elder shaman always taught the new shaman what to do. It was the duty of the shaman to doctor the Mokie when they were sick, and to keep their eyes turned to the tops of the mountains, where their ancestors watched over them. And so, the villagers were happy and peaceful. They planned on living the way they always had...

The black wolf signaled the birth of each new shaman. Everyone in the village had animal teachers and companions, but only the shaman was under the protection of the black wolf. Down through all of their generations, after each new shaman was born, the animals that would be his companions and teachers had entered the birth lodge, led by the black wolf. They walked in slow circles around the new Shaman, sniffing him and looking him over. Then some of them left on silent feet, while others stayed.

It had been told that one of the shamans of long ago had been born in the spring, and a black wolf mother and her baby had attended his birth. The wolf mother had watched as her baby had licked the feet and face of the new shaman before they turned and left the birth lodge.

But time passed, and no new shaman was born to take the place of the current shaman. The Mokie watched for the signs at each birth that took place in the village, but the black wolf and the other animals that lived in the forest never came to the birth lodge.

The Mokie's only shaman grew older and older, and still, no new shaman was born to take his place. He had no one to teach the path of the shaman to. The people grew more and more worried. The shaman was worried, too. He was afraid that all he knew would die with him.

The old shaman lived as long as he could, but he finally had to give up, and pass on into the spirit world.

The people gathered at his lodge and mourned, for they had admired and loved him. There was no new Shaman to do the death rituals that needed to be done for him, so they did the best they could. They washed and painted the old Shaman, and dressed him in his formal clothes. Then they wrapped him in his best blanket.

The men carried him to his favorite place at the end of the valley, and carefully placed him up on the tall platform they had built for him to rest on. The old Shaman lay on his high, airy bed, peacefully looking up at the sky.

The Mokie tied bags of cornmeal, herbs, water, and dried meat to the four corners of the tall poles holding up the burial platform. They chanted the death prayers for the old Shaman, and asked his Spirit to still guide them as best it could. The animals that had lived with him cried and sang and howled out their goodbyes to him before they disappeared back into the forest.

The Mokie looked at each other. What would they do now, without a Shaman to lead them? They had never been without one before. Now the Mokie were left on their own. None of them knew what to do. They had never been without a Shaman as long as their generations had existed. Puzzled, they silently went home.

A quiet summer passed. Fall set in. The air cooled and dried. It blew over the long grass, and turned it brown and brittle. The Mokie gathered their crops. After they were done with the harvest, they decided to choose a temporary Shaman to take the old one's place until the black wolf chose another one for them. That was all they could think of to do.

They chose a fine young man who was good and kind, but he was not fierce and thoughtful, and he had very few animal companions and teachers. He was willing, but some things he knew, and most things he didn't. He did not know how to make the sacred birth rattles that were made by the Shaman and given to each child when they were born.

The rattles were important to the People. Without them, they believed that the child would not know the proper rhythms to live by, and would live in chaos instead.

Their new Shaman forgot to watch the Moon so he could gather the Mokie together for the rituals that had always laid the foundation for their lives. When he did remember, he danced and told silly stories with no meaning. Pretty soon, no one went to the gatherings any more, and they ended, and became a part of the past.

And so it followed that the young Mokie growing up in the village became restless, because there were no meaningful rituals to help them understand their purpose in life. Roots and purpose grow together, and without the rituals their fertilizer provided, the roots that held the young Mokie in the little village grew weaker and weaker.

After awhile, a few of the young Mokie banded together and started exploring the mountains that hid their isolated little valley from the rest of the world. They explored farther and farther away from the village until at last, they crossed the mountains and discovered the cities on the other side. To the older Mokie's dismay, the young Mokie began crossing the mountains and settling in the cities.

The young Mokie became very busy and important, keeping up with all of the changes going on in the outer world. They began reading newspapers and driving cars, and living in perfectly square houses with little rooms in them. Some of them even had telephones put in.

Pretty soon, the young Mokie who had crossed the mountains stopped speaking of their ancestors, and of their relatives hidden far away inside the ring of tall, green mountains.

They chose to forget about them, for they were learning what shame was from the people living in the cities, who insisted they change and be just like them.

To fit in with the city people, they told themselves that the stories they had heard about their ancestor's ways were part of a past that would never return. Those ways were not needed any more, and, they had nothing to do with the way they chose to live now.

None of them had grown up listening to the magic of a Shaman's voice recounting the stories of their ancestor's strengths and weaknesses while they sat around a night fire. None of them had danced around the fire or learned to sing the sacred songs, or speak the sacred words.

So the beautiful, handsome young Mokie lived in the cities, wearing ties that choked them, and reading books that didn't make sense, and learning how to order food quickly from their car windows. They walked on concrete, and shook hands with the city people, who stared at them, and they took the mayor and the city council as their shaman and elders.

The People in the cities never went near the Green Mountains. They were afraid of them.

In the past, many greedy developers had ventured to the cities to take the mountains over. They had intended to make the mountains into ski lodges and other civilized things. But all of them had returned in a hurry from the green forests on the sides of the mountains, carrying frightful tales of all of the strange and awful things that had happened to them.

They said that black wolves had howled at them in broad daylight. Strange things had laughed at them from the darkness of the trees. The woods were full of uncivilized sounds none of them had ever heard before and never wanted to hear again. The underbrush had grown thicker and thicker until it shut their advances out, and each one had been forced to turn back.

All of them had returned, feeling frightened and put upon, as if something they wanted and had a right to, had been denied to them. They told everyone they encountered that the Green Mountains were haunted, and to stay away from them.

Besides, no one knew who owned them anyway. There was a constant fight going on between the indigenous people and the developers about ownership that looked like it would stay in the courts for at least two hundred years.

The developers went to the young Mokie who had crossed the mountains and settled in the cities. They complained about what had happened to them, and demanded an explanation. The young Mokie just shrugged their shoulders, and didn't say anything.

The developer's insatiable hunger remained, and so they turned back to the growing city. They ignored the mountains, and began to give themselves new titles, and took the land that lay in other directions.

The Mokie left in the little village mourned the loss of the young people who had crossed the Green Mountains and never returned. They gathered together in the sacred circle and wailed and cried. Their salt tears were so many that they wet the ground of the sacred circle and stopped the grass from growing. It became bare and salted ground, a place to go and grieve.

The village elders prayed every day for a shaman to help them bring back the old ways. They did not want any more of their children to grow up and leave the little village.

A long time passed before the moon's omen's foretold the birth of a new shaman.

Then two children were born in the village on the same day. Led by two black wolves, many animals came and ringed the outside of the birth lodge.

Then Tacalon, the brown hawk, and Eilion, the small black eagle, flew in the door of the birth lodge and lit on the rafters. They screeched to each other in large voices and then settled down on the rafters to wait.

After the children were born, animals streamed into the lodge behind the two black wolves and circled the two infants. Then some of the animals stayed, while others left.

Tacalon, the brown hawk and Eilion, the small black eagle, flew down from their high perches and walked circles around both babies and announced their claims on them. Their harsh cries made the infants laugh. They reached out their hands towards Tacalon, the brown hawk, and Eilion, the small black eagle.

The Mokie made a great feast and celebrated, for now they had not just one, but two shaman children in their village. And one of them was a female.

It was the Mokie custom that shaman children had to name themselves when they were older. The Mokie called the boy We-onkta, their word for boy, and Payshu, their word for girl.

The two Shaman children were healthy and grew fast. Tacalon and Eilion were their constant companions as they learned to walk, and then run about the village.

The shaman children had no shaman to take them in hand, so the village grandmothers made them drums, and taught them the old songs and how to beat old and new songs into the drums. They taught them cleanliness and all they knew about herbs, remedies and ointments, and how to remain wise.

The village elders were all old men. They held long meetings with the shaman children. The old men looked off into the distance between long silences, and spoke as learnedly as they could to the patiently waiting shaman children.

The rest of the men taught them fishing and hunting and swimming, and told them the legends of the forests and the Green Mountains surrounding them.

Before long, the other children living in the village wanted to learn the ways that We-onkta and Payshu were learning. They stopped thinking every minute about leaving when they grew up, and began to spend their time learning the traditional ways that were being taught in the village again.

Time passed until We-onkta and Payshu were almost twelve years old. It was the age that the initiation into the shaman's path had always been given to the next shaman of the village. Now there were two Shaman children in the village, but no Shaman to do the proper ceremonies for them.

We-onkta and Payshu turned to Tacalon, the brown hawk, and Eilion, the small black eagle, and asked them to find someone to teach them the ways of the shaman.

Tacalon and Eilion listened to them and flew away. They flew far and wide in their search for the rest of the summer. They were gone so long that the people began to think that Tacalon and Eilion had deserted the two children, and that maybe they were not shaman children after all.

All hope that a shaman might lead their village once again, left them. They grew sad and stopped cleaning their houses and tending their crops of beans, squash, and corn. When the men went hunting for game to put up for the winter, they had a hard time finding any in the forests. Soon, the Mokie began quarreling among themselves.

We-onkta and Payshu silently helped their families prepare for the long winter ahead. Winter set in. The freezing cold came and stayed. The Mokie people huddled sullenly around their meager fires and endured their lives...

14

Then one evening, after the moon had risen like a large golden coin in the sky, a large black crow swooped through the middle of the village with Tacalon, the brown hawk, and Eilion, the small black eagle, following behind it.

The big, noisy crow squawked and wheeled and circled through the village. The Mokie heard the crow's loud voice, and came out of their lodges. They watched as the crow landed on a neglected, empty old lodge down by the stream. The lodge had once belonged to one of the young Mokie that had crossed the mountains and never returned.

The People watched the crow strut across the roof of the tattered, run down lodge. The crow picked at the ragged door hides until they fell off. Then it flew into the hut, scattering snow everywhere. The crow fussed busily and importantly while it squawked and flew in and out of the old lodge.

After awhile, the Mokie went back inside of their lodges. They had no idea what the crow was doing, and they weren't interested enough stay out in the cold night to find out.

The weather stayed clear and cold the next day. The large black crow flew in and out of the village, loudly quarreling and fussing and making the lodge its home.

15

It squawked as it skimmed over the heads of the Mokie, carrying pieces of straw and other things in its beak or claws to the empty lodge.

That night, just before dark, a fierce blizzard began to blow through the village. The Mokie huddled around their fires. Then they heard the crow announcing something in a loud voice. They went outside to see what it was. The snow was so thick that they could barely see the black crow as it flew through the village, quarreling at the tall man following it.

The man was wrapped up in animal skins, and he was bickering loudly with the crow. He didn't look left or right at the Mokie, who had come out of their lodges and were staring at him.

The man followed the crow until they reached the empty hut. Then they both disappeared inside of it. A short time later, the man came out again, hung a hide over the door, and disappeared back inside.

Dawn came. The wind from the blizzard was still howling. The snow was blowing so thick the Mokie could barely see. They huddled in their lodges and imagined a strange thing. They imagined that they heard the voice of a shaman calling in the day, like the shaman's had done in their village in the old days.

The blizzard howled through the village all day. That night, they imagined that they heard the voice of a shaman calling in the night.

The blizzard lasted three more days. The Mokie came out of their lodges to discover that the crow and the tall, thin man had moved their few belongings into the falling down lodge down by the stream. The people crept closer to see what they could see, but the crow flew out of the lodge and attacked them.

No one knew where the black crow and the man had come from. He stayed away from the people and minded his own business. But Tacalon, the brown hawk, and Eilion, the small black eagle, kept calling out to him and walking circles around his lodge.

The Mokie watched them and looked at each other. That was enough of a sign for them, and they dutifully carried fire and meat to the strangers lodge and set it outside. Their new shaman made himself at home in the lodge, and the Mokie listened to him calling in the day and the night at dawn and dusk.

The winter passed. Their strange new shaman and his crow stayed near their lodge, and the Mokie kept them in cornmeal and meat. The sound of their new shaman's chanting and singing heartened and comforted them, and they became happy again.

Spring came and the shaman took his bow and arrows and knife, and followed the men into the green forests when they went hunting. He taught them the old ways of taking only what was needed, and how to thank the animal's spirit for giving up its body as meat for the men, women, and children.

Then the shaman went to the grandmother's and reminded them of how the food should be prepared and cooked. The grandmothers sharpened their blades and cleaned the meat properly once again with fresh, clean water and prayers, just as they had been taught long ago when they were girls. Then the grandmother's taught the younger women how it should be done…

The shaman called the people together and told them to begin their spring cleansing ritual. The Mokie went home and cleaned their lodges and everything they owned. They carried away the things they no longer needed. They swept the ground outside their lodges with rakes and brooms until it was soft and velvety black and red, and brown.

Then they oiled their lodge door skins down with rich, fragrant fish fat. They repaired their moccasins and used dried herbs, barks, and berries to dye their clothes back to the bright colors they loved so much. They washed their hair until it was shiny, and cleaned their bodies before putting on their ceremonial clothing. Then they placed their belongings in neat rows inside and outside of their lodges, and waited for the shaman.

The shaman went from lodge to lodge, smudging their belongings and their lodges. He sang and chanted and fanned his mysterious herb smoke over everything. He rattled and banged and made a lot of noise and tossed their things about.

Then he rubbed out their drinking cups with a root from the leather pouch he carried around his waist. He filled their cups with a mysterious, dark, cleansing brew he had made, and ordered the people to put their things back together in a different way. The people drank, and knew they could begin once again. The bad time was over.

Spring was short, and summer came. Once again the Mokie planted their crops and went into the forests, and gathered fresh herbs for medicines and for flavoring their food...

One summer night the shaman built a fire in the sacred circle. He built the fire exactly like the village shaman before him had always done. The Mokie gathered around the fire in the sacred circle. They told their stories, as they had in the days of old. Many animals came and sat around the fire with the Mokie. The shaman sat with his own animals and the black wolf and the black crow came and listened to their stories.

The next day, the shaman began to make the sacred birth rattles for all of the Mokie that didn't have one. He made birth rattles for everyone except We-onkta and Payshu. They wondered why he had left them out, but they didn't dare ask him anything.

One day, the shaman left the quarrelsome black crow to watch over their lodge, and disappeared into the Green Mountains. Day after day went by, but the shaman did not return to the village.

We-onkta and Payshu had waited patiently for him to notice them ever since he had moved into the village. They had followed him at a distance wherever he went, but he had ignored them. They knew many of his habits. They knew that he quarreled with the black crow all of the time, and that he talked constantly with the animals that came to his lodge.

20

He wouldn't talk to any of the Mokie people unless he had a ritual to do, or something to teach them.

When he disappeared into the woods and didn't return, they grew afraid that he would never come back, and they would never learn the shaman's way. Swiftly they packed up everything they needed and hurried into the forest to find him. When they found him, they would ask him to be their teacher. Tacalon, the brown hawk, and Eilion, the small black eagle, winged their way ahead of them into the dense, shadowy forest.

After a few days of diligent searching, they discovered the shaman sitting on a mossy ledge above a small, playful waterfall. He was swinging his legs over the water and eating a piece of meat. He looked liked he had just had a long bath, and enjoyed it thoroughly. He looked happy, rested, and relaxed.

We-onkta and Payshu were not in a good mood. They were hot and hungry. They were worried, tired, and angry. The shaman motioned to them, and pointed to a place under a large shade tree nearby. They stared at the small camp fire and the two bark plates sitting on a stump near it.

The plates were filled with tender, browned meat, and some kind of green vegetable. They were both very hungry.

All they had brought with them were a few corn cakes because they were easy to carry, and they had expected to find him days ago.

As they ate, they realized that the shaman had known that they would follow him. He had probably known where they were all the time, and had finally let them find him.

They finished eating and went to the little waterfall and washed up. The shaman ignored them. The water felt cool and fresh in the hot, still forest, but they were still very angry and thinking hard.

They looked at each other. It was time to ask him why he hadn't given them the birth rattles they were entitled to. They were shaman children after all, and he was supposed to teach them, that was all there was to it!

They turned around just in time to see him disappear into the forest again. They had no one else to teach them, so they gathered up their things, and ran after him.

They followed him everywhere he went. Every time he turned around, they were there. When they spoke to him or tried to ask him a question, he turned his back to them.

They trailed along behind him as he searched the mountains for roots, game, herbs, and many other things.

Long nights passed with the stars twinkling high above his camp fire in the thick dark forests on the high Green Mountains. We-onkta and Payshu were tired all of the time. They had to make their own camp fires and cook the meat and berries they hunted and gathered during the day while they followed him around.

At night they made their beds close enough to his camp so they could watch him in case he tried to slip away from them again. They took turns sleeping while the shaman sat up late, watching his fire and listening to the night. When he did go to sleep, he snored so loudly that he kept both of them awake.

The shaman finally spoke to them. He put them to work fetching and carrying for him. He traveled less and less each day. Pretty soon, he was laying around and ordering them to wait on him all the time. They fetched his water and handed it to him, and hunted his food for him and cooked it. They laid out his sleeping skins and made lodges out of branches to cover him at night. He ordered them to keep the fire burning all night to keep him from getting cold, even though it was summer.

During the day he wandered around, collecting plants and bark and other odd things that they had to carry for him. He borrowed their sleeping hides to make his bed softer at night, and they had to gather pine boughs to sleep on.

They bore his ways, stoically waiting on him, for they had discussed the matter, and believed that he was just testing them. But at last they had endured enough. They began to grumble about him to each other. They were tired of staying awake all night, cooking and tending the fire for him, and carrying his things around for him all day long. And whenever they asked him questions, he told them the same silly crow stories over and over again.

The shaman started getting up later and later in the mornings. After he got up, he stretched his long, thin bones and popped his joints loudly and complained about how old he was getting. Then he stopped taking baths and combing his hair. He became absentminded and wandered through the woods, making all kinds of noises, disturbing the plants and scaring the animals away.

We-onkta and Payshu were both disgusted and dumbfounded by his behavior. It took every skill they had ever learned for them to keep on following him. Still, they persevered. We-onkta hunted their food and Payshu made the fire and cooked. They listened with respect to all the shaman had to say, even though he talked on for hours about nothing that meant anything.

After weeks of serving the shaman and following him through the mountains, they finally gave up on him. They were both homesick for the Mokie, and wished they had never followed him into the mountains.

They secretly decided to return to the village. Each day, they led him a little closer back to the village without him ever knowing what they were doing.

Early one morning, they woke up to discover that the shaman wasn't in camp. They searched all over, and found him sitting on top of a knoll overlooking their little village.

He was contemplating a blade of grass. They sat down in front of him and waited. He turned his attention from the blade of grass, and stared at them for awhile. Abruptly, he ordered them to return to the village, and tell the people that he would be there soon.

They gathered up their belongings and ran down the mountain to the village. Everyone was glad to see them. They told the Mokie that the shaman would soon be there. The people laughed and put on their best clothes and started cooking. In a short time, the drumming to invite the shaman into the village began.

The shaman strolled into the village in the late afternoon. He walked tall and straight and proud. We-onkta and Payshu stared at him. He wasn't limping or complaining or doing any of the things he had done with them in the mountains.

The shaman walked through the little village without a look to the left or the right, and disappeared into his lodge down by the stream. The people waited, and in a little while, he came out, painted and dressed in his ceremonial feathers and robes.

The Mokie followed him to the sacred circle in the middle of the village. Many of them carried mysterious bundles of different sizes.

The shaman led We-onkta and Payshu to the center of the circle. He watched the sun closely while he spoke to the Mokie. He spoke of blades of grass and how they spread and grow and take root. He spoke of how he had once been to a big city, and how he had seen grass growing out of the cracks in the sidewalks in the darkest, most hopeless parts of the city.

The sun began setting, and the shaman stopped talking. He motioned to the drummers to begin drumming. Then he called in the wind. The wind came swiftly and whirled around the shaman and the two Shaman children. The wind shut out the familiar little village, and the sound of the drums.

When the wind stopped, We-onkta and Payshu opened their eyes and looked around. They were standing in an ancient forest.

The shaman took two rattles from the leather pouch at his side and handed one to each of them. Then he led them through the forest, dancing and singing. Many animals came and walked with them.

He ordered the two shaman children to hold their rattles up to the sky. The sun and the wind and the rain and the earth poured beautiful stories into their rattles.

After awhile, he led them to a narrow bridge. Far beneath the thin rope bridge rushed deep, dark water. Suddenly a fierce wind swept across the bridge, causing it to rattle and sway.

The shaman ran lightly across the bridge and motioned for them to follow him. They were afraid until Tacalon, the brown hawk, and Eilion, the small black eagle, flew across the bridge.

They ran across the bridge. Just as they reached the other side, the wind whirled around them and when it stopped, they were standing back in their village. In their hands they held the rattles the shaman had given them on their journey.

The shaman spoke to the people again. He said

that their lives and their children's lives and their ancestor's lives were like their birth rattles. The time would come when they would break open, and the ideas that were inside of them would fly and walk and be carried away by the wind, water, and sun to where they needed to be on the earth. And they would survive, just as the grass had survived in the sidewalks in the great city he had once seen.

The Mokie wept, for they knew the shaman was talking about all of the children they had lost to the cities on the other side of the Green Mountains.

Then the shaman motioned to We-onkta and Payshu, and they held up their new rattles and began to dance. A new time was beginning in the little village. The sounds of rain and waterfalls and feet dancing on the earth poured from their rattles. Painted ancients and animals rose to the surface of their rattles. The people heard the voices of their elders murmuring once more in the ancient little village, back when time was understood differently.

The Mokie stood up and sang along with the voices. They danced up to We-onkta and Payshu and uncovered their bundles. Inside of them were new moccasins with intricate beading and clothes made of the finest, soft, animal skins. There were leggings and pouches and feathers and quills for the two new shamans to celebrate their initiations in!

When the feast was ready, the people celebrated We-onkta and Payshu's coming of age ceremony. Everyone talked and laughed and ate. They danced and told the old stories of their ancestor's courage, and the funny things they had done.

A full, golden moon rose high above the little village, and at last, everyone fell asleep.

When the people woke up the next morning, the shaman was gone again. They were not surprised.

We-onkta and Payshu carried their rattles to all of the people in the village and gathered their stories into them. When they were finished, they placed the rattles on the sacred altar in the central lodge.

The people's mourning for the loved ones that had crossed the mountains to live in the cities, grew less because each of their loved ones now had a spirit place in the central lodge. Spirit would take care of them from there.

The young Mokie who had crossed the mountains to live in the cities, began to dream good dreams about their little village hidden high in the Green Mountains. They remembered their

29

ancestors once again, and thought more kindly of them. The Mokie left behind in the little village grew wiser and merrier, and trod the green grass in the valley and mountains lightly...

The years passed and the shaman taught We-onkta and Payshu well. He put them out on vision quest so they could bring back their names and have families.

The Shaman lived on in the little village until he was very old and crabby. We-onkta and Payshu, for he always called them that, took care of him as best as he would let them.

The Mokie were glad his lodge was far away from the rest of them, for animals and spirits visited him often. They heard the howls of the black wolf and the quarrelsome crow, and the growls of the bear that came from his lodge at night.

One day, the Mokie watched as the spirit of the old shaman left his lodge and walked through the village. He walked tall and proud and straight, looking neither to the left or right. Black wolf and brown bear walked in front of him, and black crow and a stream of other animals followed behind him.

The Mokie dropped what they were doing, and pressed back against their lodges, and waited for the old shaman and his animals to pass through the village. When all of them had disappeared into the forest, the people ran to the old shaman's lodge.

The women sprinkled cornmeal outside of his lodge door, and sang the songs of passage. The men built him a burial platform under his favorite tree up on a knoll above the village.

We-onkta and Payshu cleaned him and painted him, and dressed him in his ceremonial finery. Then they wrapped his best blanket around him and did the passage rituals over him. The men carried him to the burial platform and placed him upon it. They tied the things he would need for his spirit journey to the four posts that held up the platform...

Fall came, and the cool winds blew across the little valley hidden high in the Green Mountains. One day, the wind stopped, and snow began to fall. Large, thick flakes of pure white drifted to the ground.

The snow fell until it covered the little village, and weighed down the boughs of the tall green trees, and covered the few remaining footprints of the Green Mountain shaman.

More books by Patsy Stanley:
Addition Jones
Emerald Hawks Flight
Avalon Blues Quest
A collection of short stories titled An Older Wine
Red Leaf
The Green Mountain Shaman
The Use of Shield Energies
Sound Energies
The Spiritual Nature of Atomic Structure
Chakras Meridians and the Color Energies
The Elements
The Mental Body

www.ingramcontent.com/pod-product-compliance
Lightning Source LLC
Chambersburg PA
CBHW071137100726
47908CB00008B/2628